Silviya Rankova

Cookies for Santa

Illustrated by Sudipta Bose

For Alex and Danny

December is the very last month of the year when homes and streets exude festive cheer. Families and friends gather at their best, celebrating Christmas, Love, and all the rest.

Danny's house is also decorated, with colorful, flickering lights beautifying all the windows and the roof. Candy canes, a snowman, and golden-lit trees grace the yard. The door boasts a spectacular wreath decked with red ribbons, pinecones, and mistletoe.

The Christmas tree proudly stands beside the window, adorned with ornaments, twinkling lights, and glistening tinsel. Alex, the big brother, reaches the top to put on the radiant Christmas star tree topper. The tree fills the house with magic, hope, and warmth during the most festive time of the year.

Danny contributes by hanging ornaments and placing red ribbons on the small green sprigs. He then arranges his favorite Christmas train set to run under the tree. Olly, the kitty, observes with delight, seemingly tempted to engage with the shiny, dangling balls and string.

"Voilà! We've completed our Christmas tree decoration." Danny's dad announces.
"Now it's time for you to go to bed."
"But I want to wait up for Santa!" Danny exclaims. "I've baked some cookies for him!
And I hope he'll share them with the poor, hungry kids!"
Danny confides in his dad, settling down beside the tree.

As night descends, only the stars illuminate the sky.

Santa's sleigh dashes through the Christmas night, propelled by his cherished team of reindeer: Dasher, Dancer, Prancer, Vixen, Comet, Cupid, Donner, Blitzen, and of course, Rudolph, the red-nosed reindeer. Together, they carry a sleigh filled with gifts, spreading cheer far and wide.

The prominent red sleigh lands gracefully in front of Danny's house window, its bells ringing a joyous holiday melody.
Santa steps out, bearing a sack bursting with presents.
As he begins to unpack, his gaze falls upon a charming little boy with cookies, peacefully slumbering by the tree.

The cookies smell so delicious, so Santa eagerly takes a bite. With a warm smile, he places the gifts beneath the Christmas tree- a tow-truck for Danny, fulfilling his wish, a new set of headphones for Alex to relish his music, a snug sweater for Daddy, and an enthralling new book for Mommy.

Then, the good-hearted Santa lifts Danny in his arms, and slowly makes his way to his room to gently place him in his bed.
Just as Santa enters, Danny's older brother stirs awake, sleepily rubbing his eyes.
"I don't remember asking for a new brother on my Christmas list.", mutters Alex.

Santa smiles and waves goodbye:
"Ho-Ho-Ho! I'll return to visit you next Christmas Eve."
With that, he gathers the cookies Danny prepared, settles into his spacious sleigh, and takes off into the night sky along with the presents.

On the following Christmas morning, Danny's family gathers around the tree to unwrap their gifts. To his surprise, Danny found a message next to his cookies.

"Look, everyone, Santa enjoyed my cookies and left me a message!" Danny exclaims.

"Your cookies are the most delicious. I'll share a piece of your generous heart with everyone! Love, Santa."

"I had an interesting dream!" Alex chimes in. "I saw Santa in my room, bringing me a new brother."

"Well, that's quite an imaginative dream," Mommy responds.

"We might have to consider that for your next Christmas list!" Daddy playfully winks.

Soon after, Mommy prepares hot cocoa for everyone to savor.
Alex adds marshmallows to each cup while Danny passes some cookies.
Daddy enthusiastically signals for everyone to gather for the family's holiday picture.

Christmas is one of the most joyful holidays of the year.
A time when families gather to share food and cheer.
It's a season of exchanging gifts and singing merry tunes:
"We wish you a Merry Christmas and a Happy New Year!"

Color the Christmas tree.

Help Santa to get to the sack of presents.

WORD SEARCH

H T L V B O P L D O I S N F D
O R N A M E N T S A D T X S P
T C O O K I E S R L S A S Z A
K I M E C L K L K J E U H Q R
R B O A G I K X X Z A I S D T
Z J E T V G S V V L N M G W I
H G U D O H C T S A N T A H E
H I C H A T T H O R S U V P S
U F V J J S R L P C P O I N Q
K T N U W X E M G S K R X G G
K E B S H F E F K O P I K S M
Y R E I N D E E R I L L N N O
N R V E L V E S I L X F C G P
C C A R O L S V K R Y D U Z P
C Q C P I B L P W Q U M N H G

SLEIGH
ELVES
COOKIES
CAROLS

ORNAMENTS
STOCKING
SANTA
REINDEER

GIFT
PARTIES
LIGHTS
TREE

Rudolph the Red-Nosed Reindeer (song)
by Jonny Marks

You know Dasher and Dancer and Prancer and Vixen
Comet and Cupid and Donner and Blitzen
But do you recall
The most famous reindeer of all?

Rudolph the Red-Nosed Reindeer
Had a very shiny nose
And if you ever saw it
You would even say it glows.

All of the other reindeer
Used to laugh and call him names
They never let poor Rudolph
Join in any reindeer games.

Then one foggy Christmas Eve
Santa came to say
"Rudolph, with your nose so bright
Won't you guide my sleigh tonight?"

Then how the reindeer loved him
As they shouted out with glee
"Rudolph the Red-Nosed Reindeer
You'll go down in history."

Christmas traditions around the world

In Bulgaria, Christmas Eve is celebrated with a meal consisting of an odd number of dishes which follows the forty-day Advent fast. This vegetarian meal includes grains, vegetables, fruits, and nuts. Walnuts are a necessary component to the Bulgarian Christmas meal. Each member of the family cracks one to determine their fate for the next year. If the walnut is a good one, it is said that the year will be successful. Bad luck is predicted for the person who cracks a bad walnut. Another Bulgarian Christmas Eve dinner tradition involves hiding a coin in the loaf of Christmas bread. The person who finds the coin can also expect good luck in the year to follow.

The Christmas Eve dinner table may not be cleared until the next morning to provide sustenance for the ghosts of ancestors who may come back to visit before Christmas morning.

About the Author

Silviya Rankova was born in 1975 in the historic ancient capital of Veliko Tarnovo, Bulgaria. She graduated from Plovdiv University with a master's in biology.

In 2005, Silviya and her family emigrated to the United States in which they currently reside in Chicago, Illinois.

Silviya's interests and passion: Esoterica, Mysticism, Philosophy, Poetry, Photography, and Handmade crafts.

In 2019, Silviya published her first children's book, "How Olly Met His New family", followed by "Danny and Olly's Trick or Treat Night", "Cookies for Santa", "Fay the Maple Fairy and The Tree Doctor", "The Very Stubborn Camel", etc.

www.facebook.com

More from the Author:

They are available on Amazon in paperback,
and free to download as Kindle.

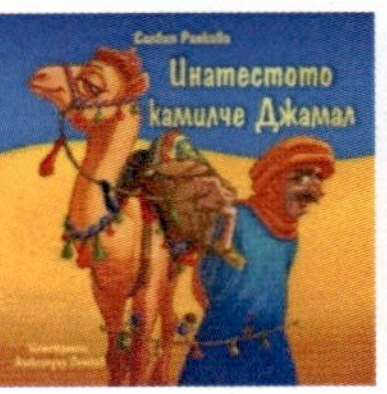

Cookies for Santa

Made in the USA
Monee, IL
29 October 2023